Pulmonary Fibrosis

A Guide to Living Your Best Life

Shankar Kumawat

ISBN 978-93-5667-741-8

Published in India 2023 by Pencil

A brand of
One Point Six Technologies Pvt. Ltd.
Unit no. 26, Ground Floor, Building A1,
Wadala Truck Terminal Road,
Near Post Office, Antop Hill, Mumbai - 400037
E connect@thepencilapp.com
W www.thepencilapp.com

DISCLAIMER: *The opinions expressed in this book are those of the authors and do not purport to reflect the views of the Publisher.*

Author biography

Shankar Kumawat is an author from India who has written several books on a variety of topics related to health and wellness. With a passion for helping people improve their lives, Shankar's writing focuses on providing practical advice and insights that readers can apply to their daily lives. Shankar understands the challenges and difficulties that come with managing this condition. In his book, he shares his knowledge and expertise on the topic, offering readers a comprehensive guide to managing the problem and living a fulfilling life.

CONTENTS

Caring for Your Lungs with Pulmonary Fibrosis

Caring for your lungs is an important part of managing pulmonary fibrosis. Pulmonary fibrosis is a chronic lung disease that causes scarring and damage to the lungs, making it difficult to breathe. In this chapter, we will discuss some tips for caring for your lungs with pulmonary fibrosis.

Quit smoking: Smoking is a major risk factor for pulmonary fibrosis and can exacerbate the symptoms of the disease. Quitting smoking is one of the most important things you can do to care for your lungs.

Avoid environmental irritants: Environmental irritants like dust, pollution, and chemical fumes can exacerbate the symptoms of pulmonary fibrosis. Avoiding these irritants as much as possible can help reduce inflammation and prevent further damage to the lungs.

Practice good hygiene: Good hygiene practices like washing your hands frequently and avoiding close contact with people who are sick can help prevent respiratory infections, which can be particularly dangerous for people with pulmonary fibrosis.

Exercise regularly: Regular exercise can help improve lung function, reduce inflammation, and improve overall health and well-being. Talk to your healthcare provider about the types of exercises that are safe and appropriate for you.

Practice breathing exercises: Breathing exercises like pursed lip breathing and diaphragmatic breathing can help improve lung function and reduce shortness of breath.

Use oxygen therapy: Oxygen therapy can help improve oxygen levels in the blood and reduce the symptoms of pulmonary fibrosis. Work with your healthcare provider to determine if oxygen therapy is appropriate for you.

Get vaccinated: Getting vaccinated against respiratory infections like the flu and pneumonia can help prevent these infections, which can be particularly dangerous for people with pulmonary fibrosis.

Attend pulmonary rehabilitation: Pulmonary rehabilitation is a program designed to help people with lung disease improve their lung function and quality of life. These programs often include exercise, breathing exercises, and education about managing lung disease.

Conclusion

Caring for your lungs is an important part of managing pulmonary fibrosis. Quitting smoking, avoiding environmental irritants, practicing good hygiene, exercising regularly, practicing breathing exercises, using oxygen therapy, getting vaccinated, and attending pulmonary rehabilitation are all important ways to care for your lungs with pulmonary fibrosis. It is important to work with your healthcare provider to develop a personalized plan for managing your pulmonary fibrosis that includes these and other strategies.

Sleep and Pulmonary Fibrosis

Pulmonary fibrosis is a condition that affects the lungs, causing inflammation and scarring that can make breathing difficult. For those living with pulmonary fibrosis, getting a good night's sleep can be challenging. The shortness of breath and coughing can disrupt sleep, leading to daytime fatigue and other related issues. In this chapter, we will discuss the impact of pulmonary fibrosis on sleep and strategies for improving sleep quality.

The Impact of Pulmonary Fibrosis on Sleep

Pulmonary fibrosis can have a significant impact on sleep quality. Patients may experience difficulty falling asleep or staying asleep due to coughing, shortness of breath, and wheezing. These symptoms can also cause patients to wake up frequently throughout the night. Additionally, the use of supplemental oxygen at night can be uncomfortable and cumbersome, making it difficult to find a comfortable sleeping position.

The disruption of sleep caused by pulmonary fibrosis can have a significant impact on overall health and well-being. Sleep is essential for the body to repair and regenerate, and poor sleep quality can lead to a weakened immune system, increased inflammation, and decreased cognitive function.

Strategies for Improving Sleep Quality

There are several strategies that pulmonary fibrosis patients can use to improve their sleep quality. Here are some of them:

Maintain a regular sleep schedule: Going to bed and waking up at the same time each day can help regulate your body's sleep-wake cycle and improve sleep quality.

Use relaxation techniques: Deep breathing exercises, meditation, and other relaxation techniques can help calm the mind and body, making it easier to fall asleep.

Avoid caffeine and alcohol: Stimulants like caffeine and alcohol can interfere with sleep quality, so it's best to avoid them before bedtime.

Elevate your head: Sleeping with your head elevated can help reduce shortness of breath and ease coughing.

Use supplemental oxygen: If your doctor has prescribed supplemental oxygen, be sure to use it as directed. The use of supplemental oxygen can improve sleep quality and overall health.

Use a humidifier: A humidifier can help keep the air moist, which can reduce coughing and congestion, making it easier to breathe.

Use pillows to support your body: Pillows can be used to support the body and improve comfort. For example, placing a pillow between your legs can help reduce back pain, and using a wedge pillow can help elevate your head.

Conclusion

Pulmonary fibrosis can significantly impact sleep quality, leading to fatigue, decreased cognitive function, and other related issues. Fortunately, there are strategies that can be used to improve sleep quality and promote overall health and well-being. Maintaining a regular sleep schedule, using relaxation techniques, avoiding stimulants, elevating your head, using supplemental oxygen, using a humidifier, and using pillows to support your body can all help improve sleep quality. Talk to your doctor about the best strategies for managing your pulmonary fibrosis symptoms and improving your sleep quality.

Alternative and Complementary Therapies for Pulmonary Fibrosis

Alternative and complementary therapies are non-conventional treatments that are used in conjunction with or instead of traditional medical treatments for various health conditions, including pulmonary fibrosis. While these treatments may not have scientific evidence to support their effectiveness, some patients find them helpful in managing their symptoms and improving their quality of life. This chapter will explore some of the alternative and complementary therapies that may be helpful for individuals with pulmonary fibrosis.

Acupuncture: This ancient Chinese therapy involves the insertion of thin needles into specific points on the body. Acupuncture is believed to stimulate the body's natural healing processes and promote physical and emotional well-being. Some patients with pulmonary fibrosis have reported improvement in their breathing and reduction of stress and anxiety after receiving acupuncture.

Herbal remedies: Certain herbs may have anti-inflammatory properties and may be useful in reducing inflammation in the lungs. However, it is important to consult with a qualified practitioner before using any herbal remedies, as they may interact with prescription medications and may have side effects.

Massage therapy: Massage therapy is a hands-on therapy that involves manipulation of the muscles and soft tissues. This therapy can help to reduce stress and tension in the body, improve circulation, and promote relaxation. Patients with pulmonary fibrosis may find massage therapy helpful in reducing anxiety and promoting better sleep.

Yoga: Yoga is an ancient practice that combines physical postures, breathing techniques, and meditation. Practicing yoga can help to improve lung function, reduce stress and anxiety, and promote relaxation. Yoga may also help to improve posture and increase flexibility, which can be beneficial for individuals with pulmonary fibrosis.

Mind-body therapies: Mind-body therapies such as meditation, guided imagery, and progressive muscle relaxation can be helpful in reducing stress and promoting relaxation. These therapies can help patients with pulmonary fibrosis to manage the emotional and psychological impact of their condition.

It is important to note that while alternative and complementary therapies can be beneficial for some patients, they should not be used as a replacement for traditional medical treatments. Patients should always consult with their healthcare provider before using any alternative or complementary therapies, as they may interact with prescription medications or may not be safe for certain individuals. It is also important to seek out qualified practitioners who are trained in these therapies.

In addition to alternative and complementary therapies, there are also lifestyle modifications that can be helpful for individuals with pulmonary fibrosis. These modifications include:

Quitting smoking: Smoking is a major risk factor for pulmonary fibrosis and can exacerbate the condition. Quitting smoking can help to slow the progression of the disease and improve lung function.

Maintaining a healthy diet: Eating a healthy, balanced diet can help to support overall health and well-being. Patients with pulmonary fibrosis should aim to eat a diet that is rich in fruits, vegetables, whole grains, and lean protein.

Staying active: Regular exercise can help to improve lung function, reduce stress, and improve overall health. Patients with pulmonary fibrosis should speak with their healthcare provider about developing an exercise program that is safe and appropriate for their condition.

Avoiding environmental triggers: Patients with pulmonary fibrosis should avoid exposure to environmental triggers that can worsen their symptoms, such as air pollution, dust, and chemical fumes.

In conclusion, alternative and complementary therapies can be a helpful addition to traditional medical treatments for individuals with pulmonary fibrosis. Patients should always consult with their healthcare provider before using any alternative or complementary therapies and should seek out qualified practitioners who are trained in these therapies. Additionally, lifestyle modifications such as quitting smoking, maintaining a healthy diet, staying active, and avoiding environmental triggers can also be beneficial in managing pulmonary fibrosis.

Preparing for Pulmonary Fibrosis Exacerbations

Exacerbations, or sudden worsening of symptoms, can be a common experience for people living with pulmonary fibrosis. Exacerbations can be caused by a variety of factors, including infection, air pollution, or exposure to allergens, and can cause shortness of breath, fatigue, and coughing. In this chapter, we will discuss how to prepare for exacerbations, how to recognize the signs of an exacerbation, and what to do if an exacerbation occurs.

Preparing for Exacerbations

The first step in preparing for an exacerbation is to work with your healthcare team to develop an exacerbation action plan. This plan should outline the steps to take if you experience a sudden worsening of symptoms. It should include instructions on when to seek medical attention, when to adjust your medication, and when to use supplemental oxygen.

You should also have a stock of medications on hand, including antibiotics and steroids, which can help treat infections and reduce inflammation. It is important to keep track of expiration dates and replace medications as needed.

In addition to medication, it is important to have a well-stocked emergency kit that includes items such as a thermometer, a pulse oximeter, and a list of emergency contacts. You should also have a plan in place for transportation to the hospital if needed.

Recognizing Exacerbations

Recognizing the signs of an exacerbation is crucial in order to take action quickly. Some common signs of an exacerbation include:

Increased shortness of breath

Increased coughing

Fatigue

Fever

Chest pain or tightness

If you experience any of these symptoms, it is important to follow your exacerbation action plan and contact your healthcare team immediately. Prompt treatment can help prevent the exacerbation from becoming more severe.

Managing Exacerbations

If you experience an exacerbation, your healthcare team may recommend a variety of treatments, depending on the severity of your symptoms. These treatments may include antibiotics to treat infections, steroids to reduce inflammation, and supplemental oxygen to help with breathing.

In addition to medical treatment, there are several things you can do to manage an exacerbation at home. These include:

Resting and avoiding physical activity

Using relaxation techniques such as deep breathing or meditation to manage anxiety and stress

Staying hydrated by drinking plenty of fluids

Using a humidifier to moisten the air and ease breathing

Avoiding exposure to irritants such as smoke, pollution, and allergens

It is important to closely follow your healthcare team's instructions and monitor your symptoms closely during an exacerbation. If your symptoms do not improve or if they worsen, seek medical attention immediately.

Conclusion

Exacerbations can be a common and serious complication of pulmonary fibrosis. However, with careful preparation, prompt recognition of symptoms, and proper management, exacerbations can be effectively treated and managed. Working closely with your healthcare team and following your exacerbation action plan can help you stay prepared and in control of your pulmonary fibrosis.

Palliative Care for Pulmonary Fibrosis

Pulmonary fibrosis is a progressive and debilitating disease that affects the lungs, making it difficult to breathe. While there is no cure for pulmonary fibrosis, there are various treatment options available that can help to manage symptoms and improve quality of life. One of these treatment options is palliative care.

Palliative care is a type of care that focuses on improving the quality of life of patients who are living with serious illnesses. It aims to relieve symptoms and manage pain, while also providing emotional and spiritual support for patients and their families. Palliative care can be provided at any stage of the disease, and it can be used alongside other treatments, such as oxygen therapy, medication, and pulmonary rehabilitation.

Palliative care is important for patients with pulmonary fibrosis because it can help to alleviate symptoms such as shortness of breath, fatigue, and anxiety. It can also provide emotional support to patients and their families, who may be struggling to cope with the challenges of living with a chronic illness.

One of the key goals of palliative care is to improve the quality of life of patients with pulmonary fibrosis. This can be achieved through a range of interventions, such as:

Symptom management: Palliative care can help to manage symptoms such as pain, shortness of breath, coughing, and fatigue. This can be achieved through the use of medication, oxygen therapy, and other interventions.

Emotional support: Living with a chronic illness can be emotionally challenging for patients and their families. Palliative care can provide emotional support and counseling to help patients and their families cope with the psychological and emotional effects of the disease.

Spiritual support: Palliative care can also provide spiritual support to patients and their families, which can help to promote a sense of peace and well-being.

Care coordination: Palliative care providers can work closely with other healthcare providers, such as primary care physicians and specialists, to ensure that patients receive comprehensive and coordinated care.

Advance care planning: Palliative care can help patients to plan for the future, including decisions about end-of-life care and other important medical decisions.

In addition to the above interventions, palliative care can also help to improve communication between patients, families, and healthcare providers. This can help to ensure that patients receive care that is consistent with their values, preferences, and goals.

It is important to note that palliative care is not the same as hospice care. While hospice care is a type of palliative care that is specifically designed for patients who are nearing the end of their life, palliative care can be provided at any stage of the disease, and it can be used alongside other treatments.

In conclusion, palliative care is an important aspect of the care of patients with pulmonary fibrosis. It can help to improve the quality of life of patients, manage symptoms, and provide emotional and spiritual support to patients and their families. If you or a loved one is living with pulmonary fibrosis, it is important to speak with your healthcare provider about the role of palliative care in your treatment plan.

Advanced Therapies for Pulmonary Fibrosis

Advanced therapies for pulmonary fibrosis refer to the medical treatments that are used when other treatments are not effective or are not working well enough. These treatments can help slow the progression of pulmonary fibrosis, manage symptoms, and improve the quality of life for those with the disease. In this chapter, we will discuss some of the advanced therapies available for pulmonary fibrosis.

Lung Transplantation: Lung transplantation is a surgical procedure that involves replacing a diseased lung with a healthy lung from a donor. Lung transplantation is considered an advanced therapy for pulmonary fibrosis because it is usually only recommended for people with advanced stages of the disease. Lung transplantation can significantly improve the quality of life and survival for people with pulmonary fibrosis who are eligible for the procedure.

Anti-Fibrotic Medications: Anti-fibrotic medications are a relatively new class of drugs that can slow down the progression of pulmonary fibrosis. Two anti-fibrotic medications, pirfenidone and nintedanib, have been approved for use in the treatment of idiopathic pulmonary fibrosis (IPF) in the United States. These medications work by reducing the amount of scarring (fibrosis) in the lungs.

Stem Cell Therapy: Stem cell therapy is an experimental treatment that involves the use of stem cells to regenerate damaged lung tissue. In this treatment, stem cells are collected from the patient's bone marrow, processed in a laboratory, and then re-introduced into the patient's body. While stem cell therapy is still in the early stages of development, early research has shown promising results for the treatment of pulmonary fibrosis.

Oxygen Therapy: Oxygen therapy is a treatment that involves the use of supplemental oxygen to help people with pulmonary fibrosis breathe more easily. Oxygen therapy can help improve breathing and reduce symptoms such as shortness of breath, fatigue, and headaches. Oxygen therapy can be delivered through a nasal cannula, a face mask, or a portable oxygen tank.

Pulmonary Rehabilitation: Pulmonary rehabilitation is a comprehensive program that helps people with pulmonary fibrosis manage their symptoms, improve their lung function, and increase their physical activity levels. Pulmonary rehabilitation programs typically include exercise training, breathing exercises, education on pulmonary fibrosis and its management, and nutritional counseling.

Clinical Trials: Clinical trials are research studies that test new treatments for pulmonary fibrosis. People with pulmonary fibrosis may be eligible to participate in clinical trials, which can offer access to advanced treatments that are not yet widely available.

In conclusion, advanced therapies for pulmonary fibrosis can help slow down the progression of the disease, manage symptoms, and improve the quality of life for those with the disease. Lung transplantation, anti-fibrotic medications, stem cell therapy, oxygen therapy, pulmonary rehabilitation, and clinical trials are all examples of advanced therapies that may be recommended for people with pulmonary fibrosis. It is important to discuss all available treatment options with a healthcare provider to determine the best course of action for managing pulmonary fibrosis.

Communicating with Your Healthcare Team

When it comes to managing a chronic illness like pulmonary fibrosis, communication with your healthcare team is essential. Your healthcare team consists of your doctor, nurses, respiratory therapist, and any other specialists you may see. They work together to provide you with the best possible care and treatment for your condition. Effective communication with your healthcare team can help you better manage your symptoms, improve your quality of life, and ensure that you receive the care you need when you need it.

Here are some tips on how to communicate effectively with your healthcare team:

Be prepared for your appointments: Write down any questions or concerns you have before your appointment. It's easy to forget something important when you're in the moment, so having a list will help you stay on track. Also, bring a notebook and pen with you to take notes during the appointment.

Be honest: Your healthcare team needs to know what's going on with you, both physically and emotionally, in order to provide the best possible care. Be honest about your symptoms, any changes you've noticed, and how your condition is affecting your daily life.

Ask questions: If you don't understand something your healthcare provider is saying, don't be afraid to ask for clarification. Ask about your treatment options, potential side effects, and any other questions you may have. Understanding your condition and treatment can help you feel more in control and involved in your care.

Keep a health diary: Keeping a diary of your symptoms, treatments, and medications can be helpful in tracking your progress and identifying any patterns or triggers. Share this diary with your healthcare team so they can get a better idea of your condition and how to adjust your treatment plan.

Use open communication: When discussing your symptoms or concerns, use open-ended questions to encourage your healthcare team to share their expertise and knowledge. For example, instead of asking a yes or no question, ask something like, "Can you tell me more about how this medication works?"

Be an active participant: Take an active role in your healthcare by asking for copies of your medical records, staying informed about your condition and treatment options, and sharing your own thoughts and opinions. Your healthcare team is there to support you, but ultimately you are the one in control of your own care.

Seek a second opinion: If you have concerns about your diagnosis or treatment plan, don't be afraid to seek a second opinion. It's important to feel confident and comfortable with your healthcare team and the decisions being made about your care.

Effective communication with your healthcare team is crucial for managing your pulmonary fibrosis. By being prepared, honest, and active in your care, you can build a strong relationship with your healthcare team and ensure that you receive the best possible care and treatment for your condition.

Support for Pulmonary Fibrosis Patients and Caregivers

Living with pulmonary fibrosis can be challenging, both for patients and their caregivers. It is a progressive disease that can have a significant impact on quality of life, and the emotional toll can be heavy. However, there are many resources available to help patients and their loved ones navigate this difficult journey.

Support Groups

One of the most valuable resources for patients with pulmonary fibrosis and their caregivers is support groups. These groups can provide a safe and supportive environment where patients and caregivers can share their experiences and connect with others who are going through similar challenges. Support groups can be found online, through local hospitals or clinics, or through organizations like the Pulmonary Fibrosis Foundation.

Counseling

Individual or family counseling can also be beneficial for patients and their caregivers. Counseling can help individuals manage stress and anxiety, and develop coping strategies to better deal with the challenges of pulmonary fibrosis. Counseling can be found through local hospitals or clinics, or through organizations like the American Lung Association.

Educational Resources

There are also a variety of educational resources available to help patients and caregivers better understand pulmonary fibrosis and its treatment. The Pulmonary Fibrosis Foundation offers a wealth of information on their website, including information on treatment options, clinical trials, and support resources. Local hospitals and clinics may also offer educational programs or seminars on pulmonary fibrosis.

Financial Assistance

Pulmonary fibrosis can be an expensive disease to manage, and many patients and caregivers struggle with the financial burden of treatment. Fortunately, there are a number of resources available to help patients and caregivers manage the cost of care. Non-profit organizations like the National Organization for Rare Disorders and the HealthWell Foundation offer financial assistance programs for patients with pulmonary fibrosis.

Caregiver Support

Caregivers of patients with pulmonary fibrosis also need support. Caregiving can be a demanding and stressful role, and caregivers may experience feelings of isolation or burnout. Caregiver support groups can provide a safe and supportive environment for caregivers to share their experiences and connect with others who are going through similar challenges. The Family Caregiver Alliance offers a wealth of resources and support for caregivers.

In conclusion, pulmonary fibrosis can be a challenging and isolating disease, but patients and their caregivers do not have to face it alone. There are many resources available to help patients and their loved ones manage the physical, emotional, and financial challenges of pulmonary fibrosis.

By connecting with others who are going through similar experiences, educating themselves on the disease and its treatment options, and accessing financial and emotional support resources, patients and caregivers can improve their quality of life and find hope for the future.

Financial Support for Pulmonary Fibrosis Patients

Pulmonary fibrosis is a chronic, progressive lung disease that can have a significant impact on a person's quality of life. In addition to the physical and emotional toll, it can also cause financial strain due to medical bills, medication costs, and lost income from being unable to work. Fortunately, there are various financial support options available for pulmonary fibrosis patients.

Insurance Coverage

One of the first steps in managing the financial burden of pulmonary fibrosis is to review your insurance coverage. This includes understanding your plan's deductibles, copays, and out-of-pocket maximums. In addition, it's important to know what treatments and medications are covered under your plan.

If you have difficulty understanding your insurance coverage or have questions about the coverage of a specific treatment or medication, you can contact your insurance company or a patient advocate for assistance.

Patient Assistance Programs

Many pharmaceutical companies offer patient assistance programs to help individuals who cannot afford their medications. These programs can provide free or discounted medication to eligible patients. To determine eligibility and apply for these programs, patients can contact the pharmaceutical company or their healthcare provider.

Government Programs

There are also various government programs available to help pulmonary fibrosis patients with their medical expenses. Some of these programs include:

Medicare: This is a federal health insurance program for individuals aged 65 and older, as well as those with certain disabilities. Medicare covers some pulmonary fibrosis treatments and medications.

Medicaid: This is a joint federal and state program that provides health insurance to individuals with limited income and resources. Medicaid covers some pulmonary fibrosis treatments and medications.

Social Security Disability Insurance (SSDI): This is a federal program that provides financial assistance to individuals with disabilities who are unable to work. Pulmonary fibrosis is a qualifying condition for SSDI.

Supplemental Security Income (SSI): This is a federal program that provides financial assistance to individuals with limited income and resources who are disabled, blind, or over the age of 65. Pulmonary fibrosis is a qualifying condition for SSI.

Crowdfunding

Crowdfunding is another option for individuals who need help covering their medical expenses. This involves creating an online fundraising campaign to solicit donations from friends, family members, and even strangers. Websites like GoFundMe and YouCaring are popular crowdfunding platforms.

Community Resources

There are also various community resources available to pulmonary fibrosis patients, such as:

Non-profit organizations: Organizations like the Pulmonary Fibrosis Foundation and the American Lung Association provide education, support, and advocacy for individuals with pulmonary fibrosis.

Local support groups: Joining a local support group can provide emotional support and helpful resources for managing the financial burden of pulmonary fibrosis.

Financial assistance programs: Some communities have financial assistance programs available to individuals with medical expenses. These programs are often offered through local charities or non-profit organizations.

In conclusion, while pulmonary fibrosis can be a costly disease, there are numerous financial support options available to help patients manage the burden. By understanding insurance coverage, exploring patient assistance programs, taking advantage of government programs, considering crowdfunding, and utilizing community resources, pulmonary fibrosis patients can receive the financial support they need to focus on their health and well-being.

Dealing with Insurance Companies with Pulmonary Fibrosis

Dealing with insurance companies can be a daunting task for anyone, especially when it comes to managing a chronic illness like pulmonary fibrosis. Insurance companies have a reputation for being difficult to work with, and pulmonary fibrosis patients may face several hurdles when trying to access the care they need.

In this chapter, we will discuss some tips for dealing with insurance companies and navigating the complex world of healthcare coverage.

Understanding Your Insurance Coverage

The first step in dealing with insurance companies is to understand your insurance coverage. Make sure you know what your insurance plan covers and what it does not. This information should be available in your plan documents, but you can also contact your insurance company for more information.

You should also be familiar with the terminology used by insurance companies, such as deductibles, copayments, coinsurance, and out-of-pocket maximums. Knowing what these terms mean can help you understand your healthcare costs and avoid unexpected bills.

Working with Your Healthcare Team

Your healthcare team can be a valuable resource when dealing with insurance companies. They can help you navigate the complexities of your insurance coverage and advocate for the care you need.

Be sure to communicate openly with your healthcare team about your insurance coverage and any financial concerns you may have. They can work with you to find affordable treatment options and help you access financial assistance programs.

Appealing Denials

Insurance companies may deny coverage for certain treatments or procedures, which can be frustrating for patients and their families. If you receive a denial, do not give up. You have the right to appeal the decision.

Start by reviewing your insurance plan documents to understand the appeals process. You may need to submit additional information or medical records to support your case. Consider working with your healthcare team to build a strong appeal.

If your appeal is denied, you may have the option to request an external review. This involves having an independent reviewer evaluate your case and make a recommendation to the insurance company.

Seeking Financial Assistance

Pulmonary fibrosis patients may face significant healthcare costs, including medication, oxygen therapy, and pulmonary rehabilitation. Fortunately, there are several financial assistance programs available to help offset these costs.

One option is to explore patient assistance programs offered by pharmaceutical companies. These programs can provide free or discounted medication to eligible patients.

You can contact the pharmaceutical company directly or work with your healthcare team to explore these options.

There are also several nonprofit organizations that offer financial assistance to pulmonary fibrosis patients. These organizations can help with a range of expenses, including medication, medical equipment, and transportation costs. Some examples include the Pulmonary Fibrosis Foundation and the HealthWell Foundation.

Conclusion

Dealing with insurance companies can be a challenge, but it is an important part of managing your pulmonary fibrosis. Understanding your insurance coverage, working with your healthcare team, appealing denials, and seeking financial assistance can help you access the care you need and manage your healthcare costs.

Remember, you are not alone. There are resources available to support you and your family as you navigate the complex world of healthcare coverage. Don't be afraid to reach out for help and advocate for your needs.

Living Your Best Life with Pulmonary Fibrosis

Living with pulmonary fibrosis can be challenging, but it is important to remember that it is possible to lead a fulfilling life. There are several steps you can take to manage your symptoms and improve your overall well-being. In this chapter, we will discuss tips and strategies for living your best life with pulmonary fibrosis.

Stay active: It is important to stay active and exercise regularly, even if it means starting with small activities such as walking around the house or doing chair exercises. Physical activity can help improve lung function, reduce shortness of breath, and improve overall fitness.

Practice good nutrition: Eating a well-balanced diet can help improve your overall health and energy levels. Make sure to include plenty of fruits, vegetables, lean protein, and whole grains in your diet.

Manage stress: Stress can exacerbate symptoms of pulmonary fibrosis, so it is important to find ways to manage it. Consider relaxation techniques such as meditation, deep breathing, or yoga.

Seek support: Joining a support group or talking to a therapist can be helpful in coping with the emotional toll of pulmonary fibrosis. Connecting with others who are going through similar experiences can provide a sense of community and understanding.

Take your medications as prescribed: Following your medication regimen is important to manage your symptoms and slow the progression of the disease. Make sure to discuss any concerns or side effects with your healthcare provider.

Plan ahead: It is important to plan ahead for exacerbations or hospitalizations. Have a plan in place for who will care for you, and make sure to communicate this plan with your healthcare provider and loved ones.

Keep a positive outlook: It can be easy to become discouraged or overwhelmed with the challenges of pulmonary fibrosis, but it is important to focus on the positive aspects of life. Celebrate small victories and find joy in the things you enjoy doing.

Stay informed: Stay up-to-date on the latest research and treatment options for pulmonary fibrosis. Educating yourself on the disease can help you feel more in control and empowered in managing your condition.

In conclusion, living with pulmonary fibrosis can be challenging, but it is possible to lead a fulfilling life with the right strategies and support. By staying active, practicing good nutrition, managing stress, seeking support, taking medications as prescribed, planning ahead, keeping a positive outlook, and staying informed, you can improve your overall well-being and quality of life. Remember, you are not alone in this journey, and there are resources available to help you along the way.

Understanding Pulmonary Fibrosis

Pulmonary fibrosis is a condition that affects the lungs and causes them to become scarred and stiff, making it difficult to breathe. This scarring, or fibrosis, can occur in different parts of the lungs and can vary in severity from person to person. Understanding pulmonary fibrosis is crucial in managing the condition and improving quality of life for patients.

The cause of pulmonary fibrosis is not fully understood, but it is thought to be the result of an abnormal healing process in the lungs. When the lungs are damaged, the body responds by forming scar tissue to repair the damage. In pulmonary fibrosis, this process goes awry and excess scar tissue forms, leading to the stiffening of the lungs and difficulty breathing.

There are several risk factors for developing pulmonary fibrosis. These include exposure to environmental toxins such as asbestos or silica dust, certain medications, infections, and autoimmune diseases. Smoking can also increase the risk of developing the condition.

Diagnosis of pulmonary fibrosis typically involves a combination of medical history, physical exam, and imaging tests such as chest X-rays or CT scans. A lung biopsy may also be performed to confirm the diagnosis and determine the extent of the scarring.

Symptoms of pulmonary fibrosis can include shortness of breath, persistent cough, fatigue, and unexplained weight loss. As the condition progresses, patients may experience worsening symptoms and decreased lung function.

There are several types of pulmonary fibrosis, including idiopathic pulmonary fibrosis (IPF), which is the most common form. IPF occurs for unknown reasons and tends to affect older adults. Other types of pulmonary fibrosis may be caused by specific underlying conditions, such as connective tissue disorders or exposure to environmental toxins.

Treatment for pulmonary fibrosis depends on the underlying cause and the severity of the condition. Medications such as corticosteroids or immunosuppressants may be used to reduce inflammation in the lungs and slow the progression of the scarring. Oxygen therapy may also be necessary to improve breathing, especially during exercise or sleep.

Pulmonary rehabilitation, which includes exercise, breathing techniques, and education on managing the condition, can also be beneficial for patients with pulmonary fibrosis. In some cases, advanced therapies such as lung transplantation may be necessary.

Living with pulmonary fibrosis can be challenging, both physically and emotionally. It is important for patients to work closely with their healthcare team and develop a comprehensive management plan that includes medication, pulmonary rehabilitation, and lifestyle modifications such as quitting smoking and avoiding environmental toxins.

In addition to medical treatment, patients may benefit from support groups or counseling to help cope with the emotional toll of the condition. Family members and caregivers can also play a vital role in providing support and helping with daily tasks.

In conclusion, understanding pulmonary fibrosis is crucial in managing the condition and improving quality of life for patients. While there is no cure for the condition, there are a variety of treatments and management strategies that can help reduce symptoms and slow the progression of the scarring. Working closely with a healthcare team and developing a comprehensive management plan can help patients live their best life with pulmonary fibrosis.

Causes and Risk Factors of Pulmonary Fibrosis

Pulmonary fibrosis is a condition that results in the formation of scar tissue, or fibrosis, in the lungs. This scarring makes it difficult for the lungs to function properly, causing shortness of breath and other respiratory symptoms. While the exact cause of pulmonary fibrosis is not fully understood, there are several risk factors that have been identified.

Environmental Toxins

Exposure to environmental toxins, such as asbestos, silica dust, or certain chemicals, is a known risk factor for pulmonary fibrosis. These substances can cause inflammation in the lungs, leading to scarring over time. In some cases, the onset of pulmonary fibrosis may not occur until years after exposure to the toxin.

Medications

Certain medications have also been linked to the development of pulmonary fibrosis. These include some antibiotics, chemotherapy drugs, and anti-inflammatory medications. The risk of developing pulmonary fibrosis from these medications is generally low, and the benefits of the medication typically outweigh the risk.

Infections

Infections can also lead to the development of pulmonary fibrosis. Viral infections such as Epstein-Barr virus and cytomegalovirus, as well as bacterial and fungal infections, can cause inflammation and scarring in the lungs.

Autoimmune Diseases

Autoimmune diseases, such as rheumatoid arthritis, scleroderma, and lupus, can also increase the risk of developing pulmonary fibrosis. In these conditions, the body's immune system attacks healthy tissues, including those in the lungs, leading to inflammation and scarring.

Genetics

While most cases of pulmonary fibrosis occur for unknown reasons, there are some cases that have a genetic component. In some families, there may be a genetic mutation that increases the risk of developing pulmonary fibrosis. However, these cases are relatively rare.

Smoking

Smoking is a well-known risk factor for many respiratory conditions, including pulmonary fibrosis. Smokers are more likely to develop the condition than non-smokers, and the risk increases with the number of years a person has smoked.

Age

Pulmonary fibrosis is more common in older adults, particularly those over the age of 60. However, the condition can occur at any age.

Gender

Men are more likely to develop pulmonary fibrosis than women, although the reasons for this are not fully understood.

Overall, the development of pulmonary fibrosis is likely due to a combination of genetic and environmental factors. It is important for individuals who are at risk for the condition to take steps to reduce their exposure to environmental toxins and maintain good overall health. Quitting smoking, exercising regularly, and eating a healthy diet may also help reduce the risk of developing pulmonary fibrosis.

In conclusion, there are several known risk factors for the development of pulmonary fibrosis, including exposure to environmental toxins, medications, infections, autoimmune diseases, genetics, smoking, age, and gender. While the exact cause of the condition is not fully understood, individuals who are at risk can take steps to reduce their exposure to these risk factors and maintain good overall health. If you suspect you may be at risk for pulmonary fibrosis, it is important to speak with your healthcare provider and undergo appropriate screening and testing.

Diagnosis of Pulmonary Fibrosis

Diagnosing pulmonary fibrosis can be a challenging process, as many of the symptoms of the condition are similar to those of other respiratory diseases. However, early and accurate diagnosis is important in order to begin appropriate treatment and improve outcomes for patients.

Medical History

The diagnostic process for pulmonary fibrosis often begins with a detailed medical history. Your healthcare provider may ask about your symptoms, your exposure to environmental toxins or medications, and your family history of lung disease. They may also ask about any underlying medical conditions, such as autoimmune diseases or infections, that could be contributing to your symptoms.

Physical Examination

A physical examination can also provide valuable information in the diagnosis of pulmonary fibrosis. Your healthcare provider may listen to your lungs with a stethoscope and look for signs of respiratory distress, such as rapid breathing or use of accessory muscles to breathe. They may also examine your fingers and toes for signs of clubbing, a condition in which the fingertips and toes become rounded and swollen due to lack of oxygen in the blood.

Diagnostic Tests

Several diagnostic tests may be ordered to help confirm the diagnosis of pulmonary fibrosis. These may include:

Pulmonary Function Tests (PFTs)

Pulmonary function tests measure how well the lungs are functioning. These tests may include spirometry, which measures how much air you can breathe in and out, and plethysmography, which measures the amount of air remaining in your lungs after you exhale.

Chest X-ray

A chest x-ray can provide an initial image of the lungs and help identify any abnormalities, such as scarring or inflammation.

High-resolution computed tomography (HRCT)

HRCT is a more detailed imaging test that uses a series of x-rays to create detailed images of the lungs. This test can help identify small areas of scarring or inflammation that may not be visible on a chest x-ray.

Bronchoscopy

During a bronchoscopy, a thin, flexible tube with a camera on the end is inserted into the lungs through the mouth or nose. This allows your healthcare provider to examine the airways and collect samples of lung tissue for further testing.

Lung Biopsy

A lung biopsy is a surgical procedure in which a small sample of lung tissue is removed and examined under a microscope. This is often considered the most accurate way to diagnose pulmonary fibrosis, as it allows for a close examination of the lung tissue to identify areas of scarring or inflammation.

In conclusion, diagnosing pulmonary fibrosis can be a complex process that involves a detailed medical history, physical examination, and a variety of diagnostic tests. Early and accurate diagnosis is important in order to begin appropriate treatment and improve outcomes for patients. If you are experiencing respiratory symptoms or are at risk for pulmonary fibrosis, it is important to speak with your healthcare provider and undergo appropriate screening and testing.

Symptoms of Pulmonary Fibrosis

Pulmonary fibrosis is a progressive lung disease that causes scarring of the lung tissue, making it difficult to breathe. The symptoms of pulmonary fibrosis can vary widely from person to person, and may develop gradually over time. In this chapter, we will discuss the most common symptoms of pulmonary fibrosis.

Shortness of Breath

Shortness of breath, also known as dyspnea, is one of the most common symptoms of pulmonary fibrosis. This can occur both during physical activity and at rest, and may worsen over time as the disease progresses. Shortness of breath can have a significant impact on daily activities, making it difficult to climb stairs, walk long distances, or even perform simple tasks like getting dressed.

Dry Cough

A dry, persistent cough is another common symptom of pulmonary fibrosis. This cough is often described as a "hack," and may not produce any mucus or phlegm. The cough may be worse in the morning or at night, and can also be triggered by physical activity or exposure to irritants in the environment.

Fatigue

Fatigue, or a feeling of extreme tiredness, is another common symptom of pulmonary fibrosis. This can be due to a lack of oxygen in the blood, as well as the strain that difficulty breathing puts on the body. Fatigue can make it difficult to carry out daily activities, and may worsen over time as the disease progresses.

Chest Discomfort

Many people with pulmonary fibrosis experience discomfort or tightness in the chest, which can make breathing even more difficult. This discomfort may be worse during physical activity or after coughing, and may be accompanied by a feeling of pressure or heaviness in the chest.

Loss of Appetite and Weight Loss

Pulmonary fibrosis can also cause a loss of appetite and weight loss, as the body expends extra energy trying to breathe. This can be especially problematic for people with the disease, as they need to maintain a healthy weight in order to support their lung function.

Clubbing

In some cases, pulmonary fibrosis can cause a condition called clubbing, in which the fingertips and toes become rounded and swollen. This is due to a lack of oxygen in the blood, and can be a sign that the disease is progressing.

It is important to note that these symptoms can also be caused by other respiratory conditions, and may not always be indicative of pulmonary fibrosis. If you are experiencing any of these symptoms, it is important to speak with your healthcare provider and undergo appropriate testing to determine the underlying cause. Early diagnosis and treatment can help to slow the progression of the disease and improve outcomes for patients with pulmonary fibrosis.

Types of Pulmonary Fibrosis

Pulmonary fibrosis is a type of interstitial lung disease that is characterized by the formation of scar tissue in the lungs. There are several different types of pulmonary fibrosis, each with its own unique causes and characteristics. In this chapter, we will discuss the most common types of pulmonary fibrosis.

Idiopathic Pulmonary Fibrosis (IPF)

Idiopathic pulmonary fibrosis, or IPF, is the most common type of pulmonary fibrosis. It is characterized by the gradual formation of scar tissue in the lungs, which can lead to a decrease in lung function over time. The cause of IPF is unknown, although it is believed to be related to environmental factors and genetic predisposition. Symptoms of IPF include shortness of breath, dry cough, fatigue, and weight loss.

Connective Tissue Disease-Associated Pulmonary Fibrosis (CTD-PF)

Connective tissue disease-associated pulmonary fibrosis, or CTD-PF, is a type of pulmonary fibrosis that occurs in people with autoimmune diseases such as rheumatoid arthritis, systemic lupus erythematosus, and scleroderma. CTD-PF is believed to be caused by an overactive immune response, which leads to inflammation and scarring in the lungs. Symptoms of CTD-PF can include shortness of breath, dry cough, joint pain, and skin rashes.

Hypersensitivity Pneumonitis (HP)

Hypersensitivity pneumonitis, or HP, is a type of pulmonary fibrosis that is caused by exposure to environmental irritants such as mold, bacteria, and chemicals. HP is characterized by inflammation and scarring in the lungs, which can lead to a decrease in lung function over time. Symptoms of HP can include shortness of breath, dry cough, fever, and chills.

Asbestosis

Asbestosis is a type of pulmonary fibrosis that is caused by exposure to asbestos, a mineral that was commonly used in construction and insulation until the 1970s. Asbestos fibers can become trapped in the lungs, leading to inflammation and scarring over time. Symptoms of asbestosis can include shortness of breath, dry cough, chest pain, and weight loss.

Sarcoidosis

Sarcoidosis is a type of autoimmune disease that can lead to the formation of granulomas, or clusters of inflamed cells, in the lungs and other organs. In some cases, sarcoidosis can lead to the development of pulmonary fibrosis. Symptoms of sarcoidosis can include shortness of breath, dry cough, skin rashes, and joint pain.

Drug-Induced Pulmonary Fibrosis

Certain medications, including chemotherapy drugs and antibiotics, can cause pulmonary fibrosis as a side effect. Drug-induced pulmonary fibrosis is rare, but can be a serious complication of these medications. Symptoms can include shortness of breath, dry cough, and chest discomfort.

It is important to note that these are not the only types of pulmonary fibrosis, and that there are other, less common types as well. Additionally, many of these types of pulmonary fibrosis can share similar symptoms, making it important to undergo appropriate testing in order to accurately diagnose the underlying condition. Treatment for pulmonary fibrosis will depend on the underlying cause and severity of the disease, and may include medications, oxygen therapy, and pulmonary rehabilitation.

Stages of Pulmonary Fibrosis

Pulmonary fibrosis is a progressive disease that can lead to a decrease in lung function over time. The progression of the disease is typically divided into different stages based on the severity of the fibrosis and the resulting symptoms. In this chapter, we will discuss the different stages of pulmonary fibrosis and what they mean for patients.

Stage 1: Mild

In the early stages of pulmonary fibrosis, there may be only mild scarring in the lungs and minimal symptoms. Patients in this stage may experience some shortness of breath during physical activity, but may not require oxygen therapy or other interventions.

Stage 2: Moderate

As the disease progresses, patients may enter the moderate stage of pulmonary fibrosis. In this stage, there is a greater degree of scarring in the lungs, which can lead to more significant symptoms such as persistent coughing, fatigue, and shortness of breath, even during mild activity. Patients in this stage may require supplemental oxygen therapy to help manage their symptoms.

Stage 3: Severe

In the severe stage of pulmonary fibrosis, the degree of scarring in the lungs has progressed significantly, leading to a further decrease in lung function and more severe symptoms. Patients in this stage may experience significant difficulty breathing, even at rest, and may require high-flow oxygen therapy or even mechanical ventilation in order to maintain adequate oxygen levels in the body.

Stage 4: End-Stage

The end-stage of pulmonary fibrosis is the most advanced stage of the disease, and is characterized by significant scarring and damage to the lungs. Patients in this stage may experience extreme difficulty breathing, and may require continuous oxygen therapy or mechanical ventilation in order to maintain life-sustaining levels of oxygen in the body. In some cases, end-stage pulmonary fibrosis may be terminal.

It is important to note that the progression of pulmonary fibrosis can vary significantly between individuals, and not all patients will progress through these stages in the same way or at the same rate. Additionally, some patients may experience a plateau in their disease progression, where the symptoms remain stable for a period of time before progressing further.

Treatment for pulmonary fibrosis will depend on the underlying cause of the disease as well as the stage of the disease. In the earlier stages of the disease, treatment may focus on managing symptoms and slowing the progression of the fibrosis, while in the later stages, treatment may focus on improving quality of life and managing end-stage symptoms. Treatments may include medications, oxygen therapy, pulmonary rehabilitation, and in some cases, lung transplant. It is important for patients with pulmonary fibrosis to work closely with their healthcare providers to develop an individualized treatment plan that meets their unique needs and goals.

The Impact of Pulmonary Fibrosis on Your Life

Pulmonary fibrosis is a chronic lung disease that can have a significant impact on a patient's life. As the disease progresses, patients may experience a range of physical and emotional changes that can affect their ability to perform daily activities, socialize with friends and family, and maintain their overall quality of life. In this chapter, we will explore the impact of pulmonary fibrosis on different aspects of a patient's life.

Physical Impact

The physical impact of pulmonary fibrosis can be significant, and may include symptoms such as shortness of breath, persistent coughing, and fatigue. These symptoms can make it difficult for patients to perform even basic tasks such as walking or climbing stairs, and may limit their ability to participate in activities that they once enjoyed. As the disease progresses, patients may require supplemental oxygen therapy or other interventions to help manage their symptoms and maintain adequate oxygen levels in the body.

In addition to these symptoms, patients with pulmonary fibrosis may also be at increased risk of developing other health problems such as pneumonia, heart disease, and lung cancer. These comorbidities can further impact a patient's physical health and well-being, and may require additional medical management.

Emotional Impact

The emotional impact of pulmonary fibrosis can be just as significant as the physical impact, and may include feelings of anxiety, depression, and isolation. Patients with pulmonary fibrosis may feel overwhelmed by the physical changes they are experiencing, as well as the impact these changes may have on their relationships and daily activities. Additionally, patients with pulmonary fibrosis may face stigma or discrimination due to their condition, which can further contribute to feelings of isolation and low self-esteem. It is important for patients with pulmonary fibrosis to seek emotional support and resources to help them cope with these challenges and maintain their mental health and well-being.

Social Impact

Pulmonary fibrosis can also have a significant impact on a patient's social life. Patients may find it difficult to participate in social activities or maintain relationships with friends and family due to their physical symptoms and limitations. They may also face challenges in the workplace, such as reduced productivity or difficulty performing job duties.

As the disease progresses, patients may require assistance with daily activities such as cooking, cleaning, and self-care, which can further impact their ability to maintain their independence and participate in social activities. It is important for patients to work closely with their healthcare providers and loved ones to develop strategies for managing these challenges and maintaining their social connections and quality of life.

Conclusion

Pulmonary fibrosis can have a significant impact on a patient's life, both physically and emotionally. It is important for patients with pulmonary fibrosis to seek medical care and support to help them manage their symptoms, maintain their mental health, and stay engaged with their social networks. With the right treatment and support, patients with pulmonary fibrosis can maintain a good quality of life and continue to participate in the activities that matter most to them.

Coping with the Emotional Toll of Pulmonary Fibrosis

Living with pulmonary fibrosis can be an emotional rollercoaster. Patients and their loved ones may experience a range of emotions such as fear, anxiety, sadness, anger, and frustration. Coping with the emotional toll of this disease is just as important as managing the physical symptoms. In this chapter, we will discuss ways to cope with the emotional challenges of living with pulmonary fibrosis.

Acknowledge Your Feelings

The first step in coping with the emotional toll of pulmonary fibrosis is to acknowledge your feelings. It is normal to experience a range of emotions when living with a chronic illness, and it is important to give yourself permission to feel them. Denying or suppressing your emotions can lead to increased stress and anxiety.

Talking about your feelings with a trusted friend, family member, or therapist can be helpful. Joining a support group or attending a pulmonary fibrosis education event can also provide a safe space to express your emotions and connect with others who understand what you are going through.

Stay Informed

Learning about pulmonary fibrosis and its progression can help alleviate some of the anxiety and uncertainty that often accompany the disease. It is important to stay informed about the latest research, treatment options, and management strategies. Your healthcare provider can be a valuable source of information and can help you understand your diagnosis and treatment plan.

It is also important to educate yourself about the resources and support available to you. Pulmonary fibrosis organizations such as the Pulmonary Fibrosis Foundation and the American Lung Association offer educational materials, support groups, and other resources for patients and their families.

Practice Self-Care

Taking care of yourself is crucial when living with pulmonary fibrosis. Self-care can mean different things to different people, but it often involves activities such as exercise, healthy eating, and stress reduction techniques such as meditation or deep breathing.

Regular exercise can improve lung function, reduce stress, and increase overall physical and mental well-being. It is important to work with your healthcare provider to develop an exercise program that is safe and appropriate for your individual needs.

Eating a healthy, balanced diet can also help manage symptoms and maintain overall health. Eating a diet rich in fruits, vegetables, whole grains, and lean protein can provide the nutrients your body needs to function properly.

Stress reduction techniques such as meditation, deep breathing, or yoga can also help reduce anxiety and improve overall well-being. These practices can be incorporated into your daily routine and can help you manage stress and anxiety related to living with pulmonary fibrosis.

Connect with Others

Connecting with others who understand what you are going through can provide valuable emotional support. Joining a support group or attending a pulmonary fibrosis education event can provide an opportunity to connect with others who are living with the same condition.

In addition, spending time with friends and family can help alleviate feelings of isolation and loneliness. It is important to maintain social connections and engage in activities that you enjoy.

Seek Professional Help

If you are struggling to cope with the emotional toll of pulmonary fibrosis, it may be helpful to seek professional help. A mental health professional such as a therapist or counselor can provide support and guidance in managing emotions and developing coping strategies.

Additionally, your healthcare provider may be able to refer you to a support group or recommend other resources to help manage the emotional challenges of living with pulmonary fibrosis.

Conclusion

Living with pulmonary fibrosis can be emotionally challenging, but there are many strategies and resources available to help manage these challenges. Acknowledging your feelings, staying informed, practicing self-care, connecting with others, and seeking professional help are all important steps in coping with the emotional toll of pulmonary fibrosis. With the right support and resources, it is possible to maintain a good quality of life and live well with this condition.

Breathing Techniques for Pulmonary Fibrosis Patients

Breathing difficulties are a common symptom of pulmonary fibrosis. As the disease progresses, patients may experience shortness of breath, difficulty breathing, and fatigue. Fortunately, there are breathing techniques that can help improve lung function and reduce symptoms. In this chapter, we will discuss breathing techniques for pulmonary fibrosis patients.

Pursed Lip Breathing

Pursed lip breathing is a simple breathing technique that can help improve lung function and reduce shortness of breath. To perform pursed lip breathing:

Sit in a comfortable position with your shoulders relaxed.

Breathe in slowly through your nose for two counts.

Pucker your lips as if you were going to whistle or blow out a candle.

Breathe out slowly and gently through your pursed lips for four counts.

Repeat for several breaths.

Pursed lip breathing helps slow down the breathing rate, improves air flow, and can help reduce shortness of breath.

Diaphragmatic Breathing

Diaphragmatic breathing, also known as belly breathing, is a technique that can help strengthen the diaphragm and improve lung function. To perform diaphragmatic breathing:

Lie on your back or sit in a comfortable position.

Place one hand on your chest and the other on your stomach.

Breathe in slowly through your nose, filling your lungs from the bottom up so that your stomach rises.

As you breathe out slowly through pursed lips, let your stomach fall inward.

Repeat for several breaths.

Diaphragmatic breathing helps improve oxygenation and reduce shortness of breath.

Segmental Breathing

Segmental breathing is a technique that can help improve lung function by encouraging the use of all areas of the lungs. To perform segmental breathing:

Sit in a comfortable position with your shoulders relaxed.

Place your hands on your chest and belly.

Breathe in slowly through your nose, focusing on expanding the lower part of your lungs.

Hold your breath for a few seconds.

Slowly exhale through your mouth, focusing on contracting your abdominal muscles to push out as much air as possible.

Repeat for several breaths, focusing on different areas of the lungs with each breath.

Segmental breathing helps improve oxygenation, reduce shortness of breath, and encourage full use of the lungs.

Deep Breathing

Deep breathing is a technique that can help improve lung function and reduce stress. To perform deep breathing:
Sit in a comfortable position with your shoulders relaxed.
Breathe in slowly through your nose, filling your lungs completely.
Hold your breath for a few seconds.
Slowly exhale through your mouth, pushing out as much air as possible.
Repeat for several breaths.
Deep breathing helps improve oxygenation, reduce shortness of breath, and promote relaxation.
Conclusion
Breathing difficulties are a common symptom of pulmonary fibrosis, but there are breathing techniques that can help improve lung function and reduce symptoms. Pursed lip breathing, diaphragmatic breathing, segmental breathing, and deep breathing are all techniques that can be used to help manage pulmonary fibrosis symptoms. Practicing these techniques regularly can help improve lung function and promote relaxation. It is important to work with your healthcare provider to develop a personalized breathing exercise plan that is safe and appropriate for your individual needs.

Exercise and Pulmonary Fibrosis

Regular exercise is important for everyone, but it is especially important for people with pulmonary fibrosis. Exercise can help improve lung function, reduce shortness of breath, and improve overall health and well-being. In this chapter, we will discuss the benefits of exercise for pulmonary fibrosis patients and provide some tips for safe and effective exercise.

Benefits of Exercise for Pulmonary Fibrosis Patients

Regular exercise has a number of benefits for pulmonary fibrosis patients, including:

Improved lung function: Exercise can help improve lung function by strengthening the muscles used for breathing and increasing oxygen uptake.

Reduced shortness of breath: Regular exercise can help reduce shortness of breath by improving lung function and reducing anxiety.

Increased endurance: Exercise can help improve endurance, making it easier to perform daily activities and reducing fatigue.

Improved overall health: Regular exercise can help improve overall health by reducing the risk of other health problems, such as heart disease and diabetes.

Tips for Safe and Effective Exercise

Before starting any exercise program, it is important to consult with your healthcare provider. They can help you determine what type of exercise is safe and appropriate for your individual needs. Here are some tips for safe and effective exercise for pulmonary fibrosis patients:

Start slowly: If you have not been exercising regularly, start slowly and gradually increase the intensity and duration of your workouts over time.

Choose the right type of exercise: Low-impact exercises, such as walking, swimming, and cycling, are generally safe and effective for pulmonary fibrosis patients.

Warm up and cool down: Before and after exercise, take some time to warm up and cool down. This can help prevent injury and reduce muscle soreness.

Use breathing techniques: Pursed lip breathing and diaphragmatic breathing can help improve lung function and reduce shortness of breath during exercise.

Stay hydrated: Drink plenty of water before, during, and after exercise to stay hydrated.

Avoid exercising in extreme temperatures: Exercising in extreme heat or cold can be dangerous for pulmonary fibrosis patients. Exercise indoors or during milder temperatures.

Listen to your body: If you experience any pain or discomfort during exercise, stop immediately and consult with your healthcare provider.

Examples of Exercise for Pulmonary Fibrosis Patients

There are a number of exercises that can be safe and effective for pulmonary fibrosis patients. Here are a few examples:

Walking: Walking is a low-impact exercise that can help improve endurance and lung function.

Cycling: Cycling is another low-impact exercise that can be safe and effective for pulmonary fibrosis patients.

Swimming: Swimming is a great low-impact exercise that can help improve lung function and reduce shortness of breath.

Yoga: Yoga can be a safe and effective form of exercise for pulmonary fibrosis patients. It can help improve flexibility, reduce stress, and improve lung function.

Conclusion

Regular exercise is important for pulmonary fibrosis patients. Exercise can help improve lung function, reduce shortness of breath, and improve overall health and well-being. It is important to work with your healthcare provider to develop a safe and effective exercise program that is tailored to your individual needs. By following these tips and incorporating regular exercise into your routine, you can help manage your pulmonary fibrosis symptoms and improve your overall quality of life.

Managing Medications for Pulmonary Fibrosis

Medications are an important part of managing pulmonary fibrosis. There are several different types of medications that can help manage symptoms and slow the progression of the disease. In this chapter, we will discuss the different types of medications used to treat pulmonary fibrosis and provide some tips for managing medications safely and effectively.

Types of Medications for Pulmonary Fibrosis

Corticosteroids: Corticosteroids are anti-inflammatory drugs that can help reduce inflammation in the lungs. They are often used to treat acute exacerbations of pulmonary fibrosis.

Immunosuppressants: Immunosuppressants are drugs that can help suppress the immune system and reduce inflammation in the lungs. They are often used to treat autoimmune disorders that can contribute to pulmonary fibrosis.

Antifibrotic agents: Antifibrotic agents are drugs that can help slow the progression of pulmonary fibrosis by reducing the formation of scar tissue in the lungs. Two drugs that have been approved for the treatment of pulmonary fibrosis are pirfenidone and nintedanib.

Oxygen therapy: Oxygen therapy is not technically a medication, but it is an important part of managing pulmonary fibrosis. Oxygen therapy can help improve oxygen levels in the blood, reduce shortness of breath, and improve overall quality of life.

Tips for Managing Medications Safely and Effectively

Follow your healthcare provider's instructions: It is important to follow your healthcare provider's instructions for taking medications exactly as prescribed. This can help ensure that you are taking the right dose at the right time.

Keep track of your medications: Keep a list of all the medications you are taking, including the name of the medication, the dose, and the frequency of use. This can help you and your healthcare provider keep track of your medications and avoid any potential interactions or side effects.

Take medications at the same time each day: Taking medications at the same time each day can help ensure that you are taking them consistently and reduce the risk of missing a dose.

Store medications properly: Store medications in a cool, dry place, away from direct sunlight and heat. Keep medications out of reach of children and pets.

Communicate with your healthcare provider: If you experience any side effects or have any concerns about your medications, communicate with your healthcare provider right away. They can help you manage any side effects and adjust your medications as needed.

Refill medications on time: Make sure to refill your medications on time to avoid running out. It can be helpful to set reminders or use a pill organizer to help you stay on track.

Don't stop taking medications without consulting your healthcare provider: It is important to never stop taking medications without consulting your healthcare provider first. Stopping medications suddenly can be dangerous and can worsen your symptoms.

Conclusion

Medications are an important part of managing pulmonary fibrosis. There are several different types of medications that can help manage symptoms and slow the progression of the disease. By following these tips and working closely with your healthcare provider, you can manage your medications safely and effectively and improve your overall quality of life.

Oxygen Therapy for Pulmonary Fibrosis

Oxygen therapy is an important treatment option for people with pulmonary fibrosis. Pulmonary fibrosis is a lung disease that causes scarring of the lung tissue, which can make it difficult to breathe. Oxygen therapy can help improve oxygen levels in the blood, reduce shortness of breath, and improve overall quality of life. In this chapter, we will discuss the benefits of oxygen therapy for pulmonary fibrosis and provide some tips for managing oxygen therapy at home.

Benefits of Oxygen Therapy for Pulmonary Fibrosis

Improved oxygen levels: Oxygen therapy can help improve oxygen levels in the blood, which can reduce shortness of breath and improve overall energy levels.

Improved exercise tolerance: With improved oxygen levels, people with pulmonary fibrosis may be able to engage in more physical activity, which can help improve overall health and well-being.

Improved sleep: Oxygen therapy can help improve sleep quality by reducing the number of times a person wakes up during the night due to shortness of breath.

Reduced risk of complications: Low oxygen levels can increase the risk of complications such as pulmonary hypertension and heart failure. Oxygen therapy can help reduce this risk by improving oxygen levels in the blood.

Managing Oxygen Therapy at Home

Follow your healthcare provider's instructions: It is important to follow your healthcare provider's instructions for using oxygen therapy. This can help ensure that you are using the right amount of oxygen and using it safely.

Keep track of your oxygen levels: It can be helpful to keep track of your oxygen levels using a pulse oximeter. This can help you and your healthcare provider monitor your oxygen levels and adjust your oxygen therapy as needed.

Store oxygen tanks properly: Oxygen tanks should be stored in a cool, dry place, away from direct sunlight and heat. Keep oxygen tanks out of reach of children and pets.

Use caution when traveling: If you need to travel with oxygen, make sure to follow airline guidelines and use a portable oxygen concentrator if possible.

Avoid smoking and open flames: Oxygen is highly flammable, so it is important to avoid smoking and open flames when using oxygen therapy.

Stay up to date on equipment maintenance: It is important to regularly check and maintain your oxygen equipment to ensure that it is working properly.

Communicate with your healthcare provider: If you experience any issues with your oxygen therapy or have any concerns, communicate with your healthcare provider right away. They can help you manage any issues and adjust your oxygen therapy as needed.

Conclusion

Oxygen therapy is an important treatment option for people with pulmonary fibrosis. It can help improve oxygen levels in the blood, reduce shortness of breath, and improve overall quality of life. By following these tips and working closely with your healthcare provider, you can manage your oxygen therapy safely and effectively and improve your overall quality of life.

Pulmonary Rehabilitation for Pulmonary Fibrosis

Pulmonary rehabilitation is a program that is designed to help people with lung diseases like pulmonary fibrosis improve their breathing and overall quality of life. The program typically involves a combination of exercise, education, and support from healthcare providers. In this chapter, we will discuss the benefits of pulmonary rehabilitation for pulmonary fibrosis patients and what to expect from a pulmonary rehabilitation program.

Benefits of Pulmonary Rehabilitation for Pulmonary Fibrosis Patients

Improved breathing: Pulmonary rehabilitation can help improve breathing by strengthening the muscles used for breathing and improving lung function.

Increased exercise tolerance: Through exercise training, people with pulmonary fibrosis can improve their endurance and ability to engage in physical activity, which can improve overall health and quality of life.

Better management of symptoms: Pulmonary rehabilitation can help people with pulmonary fibrosis learn techniques for managing symptoms like shortness of breath, which can improve overall comfort and well-being.

Improved psychological well-being: Pulmonary rehabilitation can provide emotional support and help people with pulmonary fibrosis feel more in control of their condition, which can improve psychological well-being.

What to Expect from a Pulmonary Rehabilitation Program Exercise training: A key component of pulmonary rehabilitation is exercise training, which may include exercises to strengthen the muscles used for breathing and cardiovascular exercise to improve endurance.

Education and support: Pulmonary rehabilitation programs often include education and support from healthcare providers, including information on pulmonary fibrosis, breathing techniques, and tips for managing symptoms.

Nutrition counseling: Good nutrition is important for people with pulmonary fibrosis, and pulmonary rehabilitation programs may include nutrition counseling to help patients improve their diet.

Psychological support: Pulmonary rehabilitation programs may also provide psychological support, such as counseling or support groups, to help patients cope with the emotional toll of pulmonary fibrosis.

Individualized care: Pulmonary rehabilitation programs are tailored to meet the individual needs of each patient. Healthcare providers will work with each patient to develop a personalized care plan that addresses their specific needs and goals.

Conclusion

Pulmonary rehabilitation is an important treatment option for people with pulmonary fibrosis. It can help improve breathing, increase exercise tolerance, manage symptoms, and improve overall quality of life. By participating in a pulmonary rehabilitation program, people with pulmonary fibrosis can learn techniques for managing their condition and improve their overall health and well-being. If you are interested in pulmonary rehabilitation, talk to your healthcare provider to learn more about available programs in your area.

Nutrition and Pulmonary Fibrosis

Good nutrition is important for everyone, but it is especially important for people with pulmonary fibrosis. Proper nutrition can help support lung function, reduce inflammation, and improve overall health and well-being. In this chapter, we will discuss the importance of nutrition for pulmonary fibrosis patients and provide some tips for maintaining a healthy diet.

The Importance of Nutrition for Pulmonary Fibrosis Patients

Supporting lung function: Proper nutrition can help support lung function by providing the body with the nutrients it needs to maintain healthy lung tissue.

Reducing inflammation: Pulmonary fibrosis is characterized by inflammation and scarring in the lungs. A diet rich in anti-inflammatory foods can help reduce inflammation and potentially slow the progression of the disease.

Improving overall health: Good nutrition is important for overall health and well-being. Eating a healthy diet can help reduce the risk of other chronic diseases like heart disease and diabetes, which can improve quality of life for pulmonary fibrosis patients.

Tips for Maintaining a Healthy Diet

Eat a variety of fruits and vegetables: Fruits and vegetables are rich in vitamins, minerals, and antioxidants, which can help support lung health and reduce inflammation.

Choose lean protein sources: Lean protein sources like chicken, fish, and tofu are important for building and repairing tissue in the body.

Limit processed and fried foods: Processed and fried foods can be high in saturated and trans fats, which can increase inflammation in the body. Limiting these foods can help reduce inflammation and improve overall health.

Include healthy fats: Healthy fats like those found in nuts, seeds, and avocado can help reduce inflammation and support overall health.

Stay hydrated: Staying hydrated is important for maintaining lung health and preventing respiratory infections. Be sure to drink plenty of water throughout the day.

Consult with a registered dietitian: A registered dietitian can help create a personalized nutrition plan for people with pulmonary fibrosis based on their individual needs and goals.

Conclusion

Good nutrition is an important part of managing pulmonary fibrosis. A diet rich in fruits and vegetables, lean protein sources, healthy fats, and low in processed and fried foods can help support lung function, reduce inflammation, and improve overall health and well-being. It is important for pulmonary fibrosis patients to work with their healthcare provider and a registered dietitian to develop a personalized nutrition plan that meets their individual needs and goals.

www.ingramcontent.com/pod-product-compliance
Lightning Source LLC
LaVergne TN
LVHW040031190726
843490LV00014B/2749